S0-BCS-160

Skating Dreams
The Winning Edge

Read all the *Skating Dreams* books!

#1: The Turning Point

#2: Staying Balanced

#3: Skating Backward

#4: Champion's Luck

#5: The Winning Edge

Coming soon:

#6: Coach's Choice

Skating Dreams

The Winning Edge

By Nola Thacker

Hyperion

New York

If you purchased this book without a cover, you should be aware
that this book is stolen property. It was reported as "unsold and
destroyed" to the publisher, and neither the author nor the
publisher has received payment for this "stripped book."

Copyright © 2001 by Michelle Kwan Corp.
Skating Dreams, Volo, and the Volo colophon are trademarks of
Disney Enterprises, Inc.
All rights reserved. No part of this book may be reproduced or
transmitted in any form or by any means, electronic or
mechanical, including photocopying, recording, or by
any information storage and retrieval system, without
written permission from the publisher.
For information address
Volo Books, 114 Fifth Avenue,
New York, New York 10011-5690.

Printed in the United States of America
First Edition
1 3 5 7 9 10 8 6 4 2
This book is set in 12.5-point Life.
ISBN 0-7868-1570-1
Visit www.skatingdreams.com

Skating Dreams

Dreams

The Winning Edge

"**W**e're here!"

Lauren Wing woke with a start.

Her father reached over and ruffled her hair. Lauren was too dazed with sleep to protest.

"You were snoring," her father teased.

That woke Lauren up. "No I wasn't!" she said indignantly.

"Well, maybe not snoring. But you were definitely twitching. Reminded me of an old dog I had when I was a kid. We always thought he was dreaming about chasing rabbits."

"Gee, thanks, Dad," Lauren said. "But I was *not* dreaming about chasing rabbits."

Mr. Wing laughed. "I know. Gold medals, more likely."

Lauren jumped out of the van and hauled out her skating bag and her backpack full of school-books. Her father walked with her into the soaring entrance to the Silver Springs Ice Rink. It was still so new that it seemed to sparkle, even in the gray light of dawn.

The dimly lit hallway leading to the rink echoed with their footsteps. Coach Perry was already there. Lauren knew that, not only because she'd seen the coach's battered old blue Subaru in the parking lot, but also because Coach Perry was the one who'd turned on the few lights for Lauren and her father. The coach never turned on all the lights, though, except in the rink itself. The rest of the lights would go on when the building officially opened later that morning.

Lauren's father patted her shoulder as they reached the locker room. "See you later," he said. "Have a good practice."

"Thanks," Lauren said. She stretched up to kiss her father on the cheek.

Her father's arm tightened around her shoulders. Then with a smile and a wave, he was gone. While Lauren was changing into the layers of tights and undershirts and leg warmers and sweatshirts that she wore against the permanent chill that hovered above the ice, her father would be what Lauren called Zamboniing—driving the huge machine that smoothed the ice.

When Lauren went rinkside, the expanse of blue-white ice would be smooth and perfect—just for her.

Pretty lucky, Lauren thought, with the little shiver of delight that she always got when she thought of that glistening, perfect sheet. By the time the lesson was over, she would have written her signature on it with her skates. Depending on how tough Coach Perry was that day, and what Lauren practiced, her blade marks would be etched on the ice from one end of the rink to the other.

Coach Perry was in her usual spot at one side of the rink, a mug of hot chocolate beside her, a notebook open on her lap, her pen scratching across the paper. She looked up as Lauren walked toward her.

"Hi," said Lauren.

Coach nodded and made another note. Then she closed the notebook, slid the pen into its spiral binding, and tucked the notebook into the leather shoulder bag at her feet. Only then did she look up again.

"Good morning," she said. She stood up. "You have been a champion for one day. How does it feel?"

"Good," Lauren admitted. "I could get used to it." The coach was referring to Lauren's victory at Regionals. Lauren was no longer just Lauren Wing, hopeful figure skater. She was Lauren Wing, novice Regional Champion, now eligible to compete at Sectionals.

"I think no one ever gets accustomed to it," Coach Perry said. She flashed one of her rare smiles. "But one does grow to like it. Yes?"

"Yes," Lauren said, grinning back. "Definitely."

"Well, then, if you like being the best, you must get to work." Coach Perry clapped her

4

small, strong hands together. "Let's go."

Quickly, Lauren began to do her warm-up stretches. As she did, Coach Perry reached into her black leather bag and took out another notebook. She flipped it open, riffled the sheets, and then said, "Your performance at Regionals was very good. You deserved to win. However, if we work on certain points, I think it will be even better. I want to work on extending your line, expanding the artistry you bring to the ice. . . ."

Lauren hid her grin this time. Coach Perry was relentless. It was what Lauren liked—no, loved—about the tiny, tough coach. Coach Midas, she'd been dubbed by some of the people in skating, because of her ability to teach good skaters how to be great ones, the ones who brought home gold medals.

Pretty lucky, thought Lauren again. Very few people were as lucky as she was. She finished her stretches. She took off her skate guards and stepped onto the ice.

Then, without even waiting for Coach Perry to prompt her, Lauren started the basic skating moves that Coach Perry insisted on before beginning every practice. You can fly through the air to the ceiling, Coach Perry said. But if you didn't know how to land, what difference did it make? Basics first, then flight.

At the end of practice, Coach Perry nodded. "Good," she said.

Lauren took a deep breath. Then she skated to rinkside and grabbed the bottle filled with juice and water she kept chilling on the ice and took a long, deep gulp.

"Whew," she said, lowering the bottle.

Coach Perry had already put on her skate guards and stepped off the ice. But instead of preparing to leave, she poured another cup of hot chocolate from her thermos and took a sip.

What was Coach Perry waiting for, Lauren wondered. She put on her own skate guards and stepped off the ice too.

Coach Perry patted the bench beside her. "Sit, please," she said.

Lauren sat down. Strategy, she guessed. Sometimes, Coach Perry liked to talk about strategy, or techniques or moves on which Lauren needed to concentrate in practice.

But Coach Perry surprised Lauren. She said, in her brusque way, "I think if you had lessons every weekday morning, you would benefit."

"I know," said Lauren. She didn't say anything else. She didn't have to tell Coach Perry that the lessons were expensive and her family could just afford to pay for the ones Lauren had three mornings a week now. Lauren yearned for more lessons, more time on the ice, but what could she do?

The coach nodded as though she had heard Lauren's unspoken thought. "However, circumstances will change."

Lauren shrugged in answer. Her parents said the same thing, more or less.

"I have a new pupil the same age as you. Her name is Courtney Reeves, and she is from Alabama. She is moving here this weekend to live with her aunt so she can work with me."

"That's good. For her, especially," Lauren said. She knew Coach Perry had other students, taught other skaters individually and in classes.

She'd never thought about those other skaters, and Coach Perry had never talked about them. Why was she talking about this skater, this Courtney Reeves?

"Courtney will, I think, be joining you for morning sessions," Coach Perry said. "She wants lessons five mornings a week."

Lauren blinked, as if blinking would make her hearing improve. "What?" she said.

"A slight reduction in fees," Coach Perry went on, "since I am working with two skaters at once, might mean that you, too, could be here five mornings a week."

"This skater—Courtney—is going to be joining *my* lessons?" Lauren asked. She realized as she spoke that she sounded like a kid on a playground who didn't want to share. She couldn't help it. "What if . . . but I . . ."

Her voice trailed off. She met Coach Perry's level gaze. "You will find," the coach said, standing up, "that having another person gives a new dimension to your lessons. You have someone both to have fun with and to measure yourself against. It will be good for both of you."

Lauren stood up, too. Coach Perry said, as she always did, "Until the next lesson," and walked briskly away.

But Lauren didn't move. She stared blankly at the coach's back, watching until the coach disappeared from sight. Courtney Reeves? Who was this Courtney Reeves? Had Coach Perry gone to see her skate just as she had watched Lauren before they had worked together? Had she asked Courtney Reeves to become one of her students, the way she had asked Lauren?

Lauren felt uneasy, unsettled. And, she realized with a start, jealous.

She was jealous of a girl she had never even met.

2

"Whoa, Alice. Whoa!" Rebecca Meyers pulled back on the leash. Alice, the black-and-brown dachshund at the other end of the leash, who was almost as round as she was long, strained to get closer to the overflowing park garbage can.

"Clyde! Clyde, drop it. Whatever you're eating, I know it's disgusting!" Rebecca's head swiveled and she fixed a steely eye on Clyde, the male black-and-brown dachshund, who had stopped pulling at his leash long enough to vacuum up something from the ground and chew it vigorously.

Lauren, who was walking Clyde, dropped to

her knees beside the portly Clyde and poked her hand in his mouth. With difficulty, she removed the shredded remains of a candy wrapper. "Calorie-free," she reported. "Candy wrappers have no calories." Wadding the wrapper up, she fired it into the garbage can.

Then in unspoken agreement, the two friends led the two dachshunds in a wide circle around the messy container.

"Thanks for helping me walk them," Rebecca said. "I don't like to take them to the park by myself. It's too hard to keep them out of trouble."

"I can see that," Lauren said. "Trash-can temptation."

"Dachshund dessert," Rebecca agreed. "Right, guys?"

Alice flattened her ears and wagged her tail. Clyde swerved sideways to glare at a squirrel.

"No squirrels," Lauren said firmly. "You have to be in shape to chase squirrels. And you're not, Clyde. Face it. You could pull a muscle. Or sprain an ankle."

"A paw," Rebecca corrected. She giggled.

"Both of them have lost weight," Lauren observed. "Clyde especially."

"True. Well, we've switched them to special diet dog food, and now instead of dog biscuits they get carrots or celery. I just feel bad we let them get so fat. Extra weight is very hard on a dachshund's back, you know."

"I guess it would be." Lauren had never thought about that. She looked at the long, sleek dogs and imagined their round bellies pulling against their elongated spines. It didn't sound comfortable. "Do they know they are on diets?"

"Maybe. But I think they like the extra walks. And Alice has started getting all excited about chasing her tennis ball again." Rebecca stooped to pat Alice's head. "Before now, she would just look at it like she couldn't remember what it was for."

They walked on, letting Alice and Clyde lead the way nose-first through the park. It was Saturday afternoon. Lauren had finished practice for the day and was sleeping over at Rebecca's house that night. She felt pleasantly tired and content.

But not entirely happy. After a while, Lauren said, "Monday. In two days, she'll be here."

Rebecca didn't have to ask who. Lauren had told her all about Courtney Reeves. "Did you ask Coach Perry anything else about her?"

"I tried," Lauren said. "Coach said I would see when I met her."

"Mmm," said Rebecca.

"So why won't she tell me anything?" Lauren fretted. "Like, who is this Courtney Reeves? How long has she been skating? How good is she?" Lauren's voice trailed off.

"Well, she has to be good if Coach Perry has agreed to teach her," Rebecca observed.

Rebecca had a very logical mind. Sometimes, Lauren thought, it was a little *too* logical.

Lauren sighed. "I know. But it's just so, so sudden."

"Well, you're going to have to share, I guess," Rebecca said. "Probably, Courtney is wondering the same things about you."

Lauren sighed, a big, long-suffering sigh.

She looked up to see that Rebecca was watching her, straight dark eyebrows raised.

Lauren looked away. She hunched her shoulders and kicked at a clump of grass. "Okay, okay, I'm being silly," she said at last.

"No," said Rebecca. "But think about all you've gone through to skate. And think of how much more you've gone through to skate with Coach Perry."

"So?" Lauren was being stubborn, and she knew it.

"So think of what Courtney is going through. She's moving thousands of miles from home, away from her family and friends. She's living with her aunt, in a place where she doesn't know anybody. Just so *she* can skate."

"She must be pretty good, if her family's willing to let her do that," Lauren said grumpily.

"Good. And tough. Like you. And at least you don't have to leave your family," Rebecca said.

Again, they walked in silence. Lauren thought about Annie McGrath and Danielle Kurowicki, her skating buddies who practiced with her after school at the local rink most afternoons. They had been much more sympathetic to Lauren's grouchy announcement about

14

"some skater from Alabama named Courtney Reeves."

"Triple-triple-toe-loop into an avalanche," Annie had said. "No way."

"Who invited *her*?" Danielle had demanded. "That is *so* unfair. You don't need to get up at dawn to share Coach Perry with some Alabama cowgirl."

"Cowgirl?" Annie had said. "Aren't cowgirls from Texas? Or Wyoming?"

"Well," said Danielle. "Whatever. Probably, this Courtney begged and pleaded with Coach Perry and she felt so incredibly sorry for her that she gave in. Plus she's incredibly rich, like her father owns a cattle ranch—or whatever is like a cattle ranch in Alabama, and he's offered to pay *anything* for Coach Perry to teach his little girl to skate. He probably even offered your coach her own herd of cattle!"

Lauren shook her head, smiling at the memory. Trust Danielle to come up with a wild story, true or not. She tried to imagine Coach Perry with a herd of cattle. At the skating rink. It was so silly she laughed aloud.

Rebecca smiled at Lauren. Lauren made a face.

Rebecca drives me crazy, thought Lauren. She is so . . . so . . . so . . .

Right.

Rebecca was right. Lauren let out a disgusted breath. Her best friend was right, and Lauren knew it, much as she didn't want to admit it.

Courtney Reeves, whoever she was, cowgirl or ice princess, deserved to be welcomed by Lauren, not treated like some evil trespasser.

"Oh, all right," Lauren said aloud. She let out her best, long-suffering sigh, one she learned from Danielle, the master of dramatic sighs. "I won't think terrible thoughts about her—Courtney—until I meet her. And then only if she deserves it."

"Lauren . . ." Rebecca began.

Lauren had to laugh. Rebecca wasn't letting her get away with anything. "Well, I'll be nice. Really nice. I'll try to make her feel at home. I will."

"Good," said Rebecca.

"I might have known it," Lauren said.

"Known what?" asked Rebecca.

"If you rescue dogs and cats and every stray animal in the universe, I might have known you'd want to rescue figure skaters from Alabama, too."

"Alabama *and* Pine Creek," Rebecca answered with a sly grin. Then she said, "Let's make Alice and Clyde run a little. Come on!"

Lauren bounded into the kitchen extra early Monday morning, startling her father. "Dad, come on!" she said.

He grabbed a dish towel and mopped up the tea he'd spilled on the counter. "What's the rush?" he asked. "Where's the fire?"

"I want to get to the rink ahead of time," Lauren said. "I want to be there when she gets there. Courtney. The new girl. Please hurry!"

"Okay, okay, I'm hurrying," her father said. "Just as soon as I fill my thermos with tea."

Soon they were out on the Northway, headed for Silver Springs. On some mornings, Lauren slept until her father awakened her. Some mornings, Lauren studied. But this morning,

17

she was too nervous to do either. She kept peering through the window, as if staring could make the van travel faster, the rink appear more quickly.

"A lucky break," her father said. "Having Courtney means you'll not only have a new friend, but that you can take lessons every morning." He paused and said dryly, "Lucky for me, too."

Lauren glanced over at her father. He was smiling. "Oh, Dad," she said. "Do you hate getting up every morning?"

"Nah. I'm an early bird. Besides, I don't have to go jumping around on the ice."

"True," Lauren said, with a grin. She couldn't imagine her father jumping around on the ice. She couldn't even imagine him skating. Now that she thought about it, she'd never seen him skate before. "Dad . . . you should learn to skate."

"No skating," said her father. "And no falling. Therefore, I don't skate."

"Someday, you'll have to let me give you lessons," Lauren said.

"I'll think about it," her father said. "Now, time for breakfast." He nodded at the bag that held their morning meal.

Lauren took out the food. But she ate without noticing what she ate. Her attention had swerved back to the rink, to the new girl.

She kept glancing at her watch. As the sky lightened and familiar landmarks began to slide by, she became more impatient.

When they reached the rink, Lauren burst out of the van as if her seat was on fire. "See you later," she said breathlessly, and for once hurried into the building without waiting for her father.

Her watch said she was early, but when she burst out of the locker room, she knew she was too late.

3

There on the bench near the entrance to the ice were not one but two figures: Coach Perry, sitting upright in her taxi-yellow coat, her hands holding a mug of hot chocolate, and a smaller figure, in a soft purple sweater, her red hair in a ponytail.

Lauren couldn't see her face. The girl was facing Coach Perry, who was talking. The girl's long, long ponytail bobbed as she nodded.

Seeing the two of them sitting and talking like old friends, Lauren felt the surge of jealousy rush up into her chest again.

Stop it, she told herself. Stop being a creep.

She took a deep breath and began to walk

toward them. As she got closer, thoughts whirled in her brain. *She looks so little! Is she younger? How does she make her hair so shiny? Why is she laughing? Did Coach Perry tell her a joke? Coach Perry never tells* me *jokes. . . .*

Then Coach Perry looked past the girl and saw Lauren. The coach stood up, smiling.

Lauren pasted a big smile on her face, too.

The girl stood up and turned toward Lauren. She wasn't as small as Lauren had thought. Her legs were long and strong, the muscles outlined in the black tights she wore. Bulky leg warmers of a screaming green were pushed down around her ankles, and the gloves she wore matched her sweater perfectly.

The girl's face didn't change expression as Lauren walked up to join them. She didn't smile.

"Lauren," said Coach Perry, putting her hand on the girl's shoulder. "This is Courtney Reeves. Courtney, this is Lauren Wing."

"Hi!" said Lauren. She widened her smile.

Courtney's eyes were blue, so blue they were

almost black. Her long eyelashes reminded Lauren of Rebecca's. But unlike Rebecca, Courtney did not look warm and friendly.

"Hello," Courtney said. She spoke softly.

Maybe she's shy, Lauren thought.

"Welcome to the Silver Springs rink," Lauren said. "You just got here, right? How do you like it?"

"It's too soon to know," Courtney said.

What did that mean? Lauren had never seen a face more expressionless than Courtney's.

Looking at her watch, Coach Perry interrupted the conversation. "It's not too soon to start our lessons. Ladies, if you please?" The coach gestured toward the rink.

Quickly Lauren dropped her skating bag on the bench and pulled out her water bottles. She'd brought a second water bottle today, one of the bottles they sold at the Pine Creek rink, with the rink logo on it—a skate with pinecones attached to the laces like pom-poms. She had been planning on offering it to Courtney as a sort of welcome present.

But maybe she'd wait.

"Warm up," Coach Perry said. "Slow, easy skating." She held up her finger and moved it in a circle to indicate that the two skaters should circle the rink.

Lauren fell in beside Courtney. "So you're from Alabama," she said.

Courtney said, "So?"

"So . . ." Lauren hesitated. Was Courtney trying to be rude? Lauren tried again. "So I guess it's hotter there, right? And not so much ice."

"There was a rink in Birmingham," Courtney said. "I skated there."

"The state capital?" Lauren tried again.

"That's Montgomery. Birmingham is the biggest city," Courtney said. She paused then said, like a child reciting a lesson, "It's called the Magic City. That's because it grew so fast out of nothing, about a hundred years ago. It grew so fast because of the steel mills."

Lauren didn't know what to say to that. So she said, "Oh."

They'd circled the rink once, twice. Coach Perry held up her finger to indicate she wanted them to go around once more.

Was she comparing their styles? Lauren straightened her shoulders, concentrated on making each stroke of her skate perfect.

"Silver Springs is a small town, compared to Birmingham," Courtney volunteered. "And where you're from is probably even smaller."

"Pine Creek. It's pretty small," Lauren agreed. She was trying to be as friendly as possible. "But big enough to have a rink. You can't go far around here without finding some ice to skate on. It's one of the nice things about the mountains."

"Not a new rink, like this one," Courtney stated. She had a soft Southern accent to go with her soft voice—and in contrast to her clipped, almost rude way of speaking.

"No. But ice is ice, right? In Pine Creek and in Birmingham?" Lauren said.

Courtney gave Lauren a look.

"Bring it in and let's do some stretching," Coach Perry called.

"I hate stretching, don't you?" Lauren said.

In answer, Courtney shrugged.

Fine, thought Lauren. Be that way. Right

then and there, Lauren decided two things: Courtney Reeves wasn't shy, she was a snob. And that she, Lauren, did not like Courtney Reeves, Ice Girl from Alabama, one single bit.

"She just needs time," Rebecca said, her voice confident. Lauren could almost see Rebecca's face at the other end of the phone connection.

"I think she's an Erica," Lauren retorted.

Erica was Erica Claiborn, a skater at the Pine Creek rink who, as Lauren and her friends liked to think, was obviously in the locker room admiring herself in the mirror when they were handing out nice. Her nasty remarks, the meanest of which she seemed to reserve for Lauren, were even harder to take because Erica had all the advantages that money could buy, from private ice time to gorgeous outfits for every event.

"Everyone who isn't Miss Congeniality isn't an Erica," Rebecca pointed out.

"True. Okay, so maybe she's only an Erica-in-training," Lauren said.

"Give her time," Rebecca said. "Be friendly but not too friendly. She probably really *is* shy and it'll take her some time to come around."

"You sound like someone's mother," said Lauren.

"Watch it, Lauren," Rebecca warned her.

"How're Clyde and Alice?" Lauren asked, changing the subject. "Is Clyde still leading in the weight-loss division?"

Like the best friend she was, Rebecca understood that Lauren didn't want to talk about Courtney anymore. She said, "Well, he's getting close to his ideal weight. I think the idea of being able to chase squirrels in the park has inspired him."

"Have you told him that no matter what shape he's in, the squirrel is going to be able to beat him—unless he learns how to climb trees?" Lauren asked, giggling. She was happy not to talk about Courtney Reeves anymore.

"Can you *imagine* skating without a toe pick?" Annie McGrath said. Her dark brown eyes were fixed on the hockey players straggling off the ice of the Pine Creek High School rink. Annie was referring to the sharp bump of metal at the front end of the figure skating blade, which was critical to all kinds of ice tricks.

Hockey players didn't have toe picks. Lauren couldn't imagine skating without toe picks, either. Skating without a toe pick would have turned her into an ice crash test dummy, she thought.

Lauren, Annie, and Danielle had been watching the Pine Creek Otters play hockey. Bryan, Lauren's fourteen-year-old brother, was a wing on the Otters team, which had just beat the Arlen Mills Avalanche, from the nearby town of Arlen Mills, by a score of 4–2.

It had been Annie's idea to go straight from practice to watch the end of the afternoon game. The crowd wasn't a big one, and neither of Lauren's parents nor her middle sister, Lacey, nor her youngest sister, five-year-old Lisa, had been there. Lacey had soccer practice, and both her parents were at work.

Bryan hadn't expected anybody to show up today, Lauren knew. It was, as he described it, a "routine hockey stop" for the Otters, on the way to "the Big Ice."

Her brother talked that way sometimes. What he meant was, it was a game the Otters didn't have to win to keep moving up the ladder to the State Hockey Championships in their division.

"Look. There he is!" Annie waved, her cheeks reddening and her freckles standing out.

Danielle raised her eyebrows, exchanging looks with Lauren. But neither of them teased Annie about her smash crush on Bryan—at least, not for now.

"Hey, my favorite fans," said Bryan.

"You were excellent," Annie said.

"I think so, too," Bryan said modestly.

Lauren rolled her eyes. "Good thing you haven't let it go to your head."

Bryan grinned. "One of the hockey pops is giving me and some other guys a ride home. You want one too?"

"Hockey pops?" said Danielle.

"Fathers. Of hockey players. You know. Like soccer moms," Bryan explained.

Annie giggled as if Bryan were a wit. Lauren rolled her eyes. "Thanks, hockey son, but I have my bike."

In an almost mournful voice, Annie said, "Me, too."

"I'm with them," Danielle said. "But thanks."

"Well, you can talk about my great victory while you pedal," Bryan said, with a cocky grin. "It'll be easier without me around. You won't have to worry about me blushing."

"You know how to blush?" Lauren shot back.

"And about how lucky you guys are that you'll get to share ice time with us in a few weeks," Bryan went on, ignoring Lauren to smile winningly at Annie and Danielle.

"What? Figure skaters versus hockey players?" Danielle said.

Bryan smoothed his long, straight black hair back off his face with a practiced gesture. Was he handsome, as Annie said? Lauren could never tell. He was just her pain-in-the-party, show-off, bossy, maddening big brother.

Good thing she liked him—most of the time.

"You don't know?" Bryan said. "The Otters are playing in a tournament for the grand opening of the Silver Springs Arena."

Lauren frowned. She'd remembered Coach

Perry talking about the "Inauguration Celebration" for the rink, but she hadn't paid much attention. The recreation center of which the rink was a part hadn't been finished when Lauren had started skating there a few months earlier. But Lauren had scarcely noticed. The ice was the only important part of the building for her.

She remembered now that the coach had hinted mysteriously about "big plans." But Lauren had all but forgotten about that. She'd had other things on her mind lately. "What are you talking about?" she demanded of her big brother.

"You're not listening," Bryan said. He tapped his ear. "Pay attention."

"Bryan!" Lauren said.

"The Silver Springs Community Recreation Center is now officially finished. There's going to be a week of celebration things: basketball tournaments and a swim meet and all those kinds of sports, since there is a basketball court and a swimming pool. . . ."

"I get the idea!" Lauren was ready to scream

with frustration. Even Annie was looking a little annoyed.

"So, most important, there'll be a hockey tournament to get the ice hot, you know? And . . ." He paused.

"And . . ." Annie prompted.

"And figure skating," he said. "A figure skating exhibition. Doesn't your coach tell you anything?"

"When did you find out? I wonder if Coach Knudson knows? But she would have told us." Danielle was off and running.

"Oh," said Lauren. "Is that all?" She stuck her nose in the air, as if it were no big deal.

"It'll be great!" Annie said. "We can practice our programs in front of a crowd with no judges. No worries!"

"Cool," said Danielle. "Or maybe we could try something new."

Lauren gave her brother a sweet smile. "See you later, Bryan," she said. "And we'll be glad to cheer the Otters on at the opening. After all, I'm sure you'll be the *second*-most exciting performance in the show."

4

"Is it true?" Lauren said, before she even said hello to Coach Perry the next morning.

Courtney was already there. She was always there before Lauren, no matter how Lauren tried to hurry her father out of the house. What did she do, Lauren wondered, sleep in one of the girls' lockers?

Two weeks of practice had brought Lauren no closer to befriending or even understanding Courtney. The girl was a mystery. She seldom spoke unless Lauren or Coach Perry spoke to her first. She seemed to be an ice-rink fashion diva, wearing outfits that were expensive and highly stylized—even for practice. She never seemed to change expression.

Lauren didn't try to be as friendly toward Courtney as she had been when they first met. The token gift water bottle had stayed in her skate bag.

But she still smiled and said hello and said, "Great practice," when Courtney skated well.

Courtney never said that to Lauren. She watched Lauren like a hawk as Lauren went through her moves.

She watched her now as Lauren stopped in front of Coach Perry.

"Is it true that there's an ice skating exhibition for the arena celebration?" Lauren asked. "My brother told me his hockey team is playing in a tournament here, and that there's going to be a figure skating performance."

"Oh, that." Coach Perry nodded. "Yes. I'd meant to tell you when it was all set. Final plans haven't been made, but it looks as if we will have the ice for a few hours on Saturday afternoon."

Courtney spoke for the first time. "Short program?"

"In length a short program, certainly. No required moves. But do we stick to our short programs? I don't know. It will be good practice. On the other hand, it might be fun to try something different, experiment a little. It will be a good time to try out any new techniques or moves you have in mind. No judges. Although, of course, I'll want you to skate well." Coach Perry stood up and looked at her watch, a signal that practice was about to begin.

"Who's skating?" Lauren said. "We are, right? But besides us, I mean."

"Coach Knudson is sending a few people," Coach Perry said. "I think you know who. And a few other skaters with whom I work are coming, plus some pairs skaters who live near here."

"Cool," said Lauren. "It'll be fun, won't it, Courtney?"

"Sure," said Courtney, in a voice that had hardly any excitement.

It made Lauren feel like a dope. She narrowed her eyes at Courtney, but Courtney just sat down and began to take off her skate guards and roll up her lime-green leg warmers.

"Is green your favorite color, Courtney?"

Courtney looked up. Her eyes narrowed. She said, "These are my lucky leg warmers."

"Oh," said Lauren. She'd slipped off her own skate guards. She gave Courtney a little smile, and stepped onto the ice. So much for trying to be nice.

Fortunately, Coach Perry hadn't seemed to notice what was going on. She held up her finger and twirled it, and Lauren began to circle the rink. This time, she didn't wait for Courtney.

They practiced in near silence that day. For Lauren, it was almost a relief. She didn't have to make conversation with someone who wouldn't talk. She didn't have to feel stupid when she said something and Courtney flashed her a look—for whatever reason.

From now on, Lauren thought, I am just going to concentrate on my skating.

At the end of the session, Coach Perry said, "Good practice. Very good concentration, Lauren."

"Thank you," said Lauren. She couldn't resist a triumphant smile.

"I believe that Courtney pushed you," Coach Perry said. "That's why you skated well today."

Lauren's mouth dropped open. Now Courtney smiled triumphantly. Coach Perry's eyes crinkled with amusement. "Perhaps, next lesson, Courtney, you will let Lauren push you. Until next lesson, then."

She walked away, leaving the two girls standing there.

Lauren headed for the locker room without a word. To her surprise, Courtney followed her. Usually, Courtney waited, making an elaborate show of stretching and warming down, as if she had a sign over her head that said "I don't want to spend any extra time with you."

"Didn't you forget to stretch?" said Lauren.

Courtney shrugged and started her stretching. Lauren remembered what Rebecca had said about being friendly, so she tried once again.

"Do you have any brothers or sisters?" Lauren asked. "I have two little sisters and an older brother. He plays ice kockey."

"I have a brother," Courney said without

turning around. She continued stretching. "He likes soccer."

"So does my sister Lacey. Soccer crazy," said Lauren.

Courtney turned around to look at Lauren.

Impulsively, Lauren said, "Do you have any sisters?"

"No. Just Alan," said Courtney. "He's fifteen."

"Bryan's fourteen," said Lauren. "The youngest hockey player on the varsity team. He's very good, but don't tell him I said that. He's way too conceited all ready."

"I know how that is," said Courtney. She gave Lauren a knowing eye roll.

"Do you miss Alan?" Lauren couldn't believe she was asking Courtney all these questions. And Courtney was answering!

Courtney stopped stretching and walked with Lauren to the locker room. Lauren unzipped her bigger skate bag and pulled out a towel and her bag of soap and shampoo.

"I miss Alan, sort of," Courtney said as she opened her own locker. "And my mom and dad." She shook her head and peered down into the locker as if she was looking into a wishing well. "I also have a dog, Betty Boop. . . ."

"You have a dog? What kind? I have a cat. He's gray, and my best friend Beck and I rescued him from the street. He's named Lutz." Lauren felt doubly guilty that she'd been mean to Courtney. The girl was homesick.

"Boop is a pound dog. You know, we got her from the pound. She's got long ears and lots of different colors of fur and her nose is short with a pink spot on it. On top, just above her left nostril." Abruptly Courtney stopped. For a moment, Lauren thought she was going to cry.

But she didn't. Instead she said, "Don't you have to go take a shower? I still have to do more of my cool-down stretches."

The change in her tone of voice was so abrupt that Lauren was taken aback. Then she realized that Courtney was really and truly trying not to let tears fall down her cheeks.

Part of Lauren wanted to comfort Courtney. But she couldn't. Courtney had turned away almost as soon as she had spoken. Now she bent, her back to Lauren, stretching the muscles of one calf, then the other. Her long, silky ponytail fell forward, hiding her face.

Lauren headed for the showers.

When she got back, Courtney was gone.

5

"Psych," said Danielle that afternoon as they finished practice. "She's trying to psych you out. Soften you up, then pow! She'll knock the skates right out from under you."

"Stop being such a, such a . . ." Annie searched for a word but failed to find it. "You know."

"Psycho?" suggested Lauren. She bent to stretch her own legs, thinking about Courtney. She also thought about how tired her legs were. Whew! Pushing herself that hard in the mornings definitely caught up with her in the afternoons.

"C'mon," said Annie. "She was trying not to

cry. Give her a break, Danielle. She's lonely. Who wouldn't be?"

Danielle's face took on a faraway look and she clasped her hands at her chest.

"Uh-oh. Here she goes," Annie murmured to Lauren. Danielle had a huge melodramatic streak. She lived for drama, and in addition to skating was also in the drama club at the private school she attended. Sometimes Lauren wasn't sure whether Danielle liked skating because it was skating, or because it was another way to be the center of attention.

Ignoring Annie, Danielle raised her gaze to the ceiling of the rink and intoned, "Lonely. Alone. Friendless. A stranger in a strange land . . ."

"Made even more strange by Danielle Kurowicki," Annie offered.

"Homesick for family. Friends. And most of all her faithful dog, Betty Boop. Betty, who lies alone every night outside his mistress's room, wondering when will she come back? Why did she leave me? Was I such a bad dog?"

"Stop," said Annie.

"Please," said Lauren. "I feel like crying. . . ."

41

Danielle's face brightened. "Yeah?"

"Or laughing," Lauren finished.

"Plus, a dog named Betty Boop is probably a girl," Annie pointed out.

Danielle flung her hands out. "You guys are sooo insensitive."

"You're the one who was hammering Courtney until you went all dramatic about her," Annie said.

"An artist finds inspiration wherever she can," Danielle said, seriously.

"Oh, back flip onto thin ice," Annie retorted.

Lauren bent suddenly to fiddle with her skating boot. "Don't look," she hissed. "There's Erica."

But pretending Erica Claiborn wasn't there had never been a very effective way of keeping her away. Erica skated right over, looked down her nose at Lauren, and said in her sweetest mean voice, "If you keep practicing, Lauren, I'm sure that *someday*, you'll learn to untie your shoes."

If Danielle or Annie had said that, Lauren might have found it funny. But not when Erica said it.

Lauren straightened. As usual, Erica was wearing a matching skating outfit that screamed "expensive." As usual, she looked perfectly pulled together and unbearably smug.

And, as usual, she made Lauren feel clumsy and angry. But Lauren didn't answer Erica's jab. Neither did Annie or Danielle. The three of them just stared at Erica. Erica stared back, her pale-blue eyes challenging.

After a long silence, Erica said with a curl of her lip, "You know, this is the wittiest I've ever heard all of you be. You should try it more often."

Danielle opened her mouth to reply, then closed it again. She drew her lips tightly together.

Lauren could almost hear Annie's temper starting to heat up. If Annie were a teapot, by now she would have whistled, Lauren thought.

"Hey!" Erica said when they still hadn't spoken. "I've got the *best* idea. For that event at Silver Springs Arena—the one I'm going to be skating in—you three should do a clown act. It'd be perfect for you. Trust me."

With that, Erica fluttered her fingers at the three friends and skated away.

Annie let out a long breath. "My mom says you're not supposed to hate anybody," she announced. "So I don't hate Erica. Really, I don't."

"She is *such* a scaly brat," Danielle said.

"Why does she always act like that?" Lauren said.

"Trust me, it's not an act," Danielle said. "Come on. Let's get out of here. Watching her chew up the ice is making me pukeoid."

"Pukeoid?" Annie said, following Lauren and Danielle out of the rink. "Pukeoid? What kind of a word is that?"

"Hurl, then," Danielle said. "Barf. Gag. Urp. Technicolor yawn. Projectile vo—"

"I get it, I get it," Annie said.

Lauren didn't say anything still. She was laughing. But she was also thinking how great it was to be hanging out with her friends.

She couldn't imagine practicing, day after day, without them. It didn't make her want to barf, gag, or urp.

But if she'd had to move all the way across the country and try to make it on her own—it might have.

The Three Musketeers, the Three Stooges, what did it matter what Erica called Lauren and her friends? It didn't change their friendship.

Lauren stopped. "Erica's right!" she exclaimed.

"Right? About what? Did you fall and hit your head when I wasn't looking?" Annie asked.

"No. About the clowns. It's a great idea," Lauren said.

"I don't get it," Danielle said.

"Why don't we do a clown act for the Arena Celebration? It'd be fun. And we could do it together."

"Wear a clown outfit? Me?" Danielle was shaking her head. "No way!"

But Annie was starting to smile. "All the falls, all the goofy stuff," she said. "We wouldn't even have to practice that hard!

"A clown outfit?" Danielle repeated. "Annie, think this through! Clown is not a look you want to wear in public."

"We could set it up as follow the leader, like we do now to warm up before practice. Only every time the leader fell or whatever, the others would have to do it, too," Lauren went on.

"And we could make great outfits, too. Totally nuts," Annie said. "Crazy makeup and maybe even tear-away clothes—you know, pants that rip and show bright-red boxer shorts underneath or something."

"Boxer shorts?" Danielle moaned. "You guys are serious, aren't you?"

"Serious?" Lauren paused. She grinned. "Hey, would I clown around about something like this?"

The sound of Clyde drinking from his water dish echoed through the kitchen. Rebecca looked up from her science book. "Have you been running in the backyard, boy?" she asked Clyde.

He didn't answer. He just kept drinking.

"He really is getting thinner," Lauren said. "He's leaving Alice in the dirt."

"Shhh! You'll give Alice food issues," Rebecca warned.

"Food issues?" Lauren shook her head. "I don't think dogs have food issues. Food attacks, maybe."

Clyde kept slurping. When he'd finished, he looked at Rebecca. She got up. "Again? You drank all that water again?"

Clyde wagged his tail. "Okay," Rebecca said. She refilled his bowl and sat down again at the table. "Maybe I should add some wet food to their diets," she mused. "That dry diet dog food is making Clyde into a camel or something. I mean, he drinks much more water than he used to."

"Drinking lots of water is healthy," Lauren said.

"Yeah, I know." Her eyes dropped to her science book. Then she looked up. "That's it," she said. "Great idea, Lauren."

"Any time," Lauren said. "Ah—what was the idea, exactly?"

"For my next extra-credit science report. I'll do it on water. It's everywhere. It's basic. You

47

can't live without it," Rebecca said, growing more and more excited by the possibilities. "Did you know you can go, like, weeks without food but only a few days without water? That our bodies are something like ninety-eight percent water? That . . ."

"Stop!" Lauren held up her hand. "I believe you. It's a great idea." She paused and smiled. "Did you know," she asked making her eyes wide and serious, "that ice is one hundred percent water?"

Lauren flopped back onto her bed and stared at the top bunk. She shared the bedroom with her two younger sisters, Lacey, who slept on the top bunk opposite, and Lisa, who slept below, across from Lauren. The room was crowded and jumbled with each of the three girls' things: Lisa's toys spilled out of a toy box at the foot of her bed. A soccer poster of the Women's World Cup team was thumbtacked to the wall next to a collage Lauren had made of her favorite figure skaters. A chest of drawers was backed up to Lauren's foot of the bed and another, taller and narrower, stood between the bedroom door and the closet door.

Lauren stared at the closet. If wishes could come true, that closet would be bursting, not with the clothes of the three Wing sisters, but with gorgeous skating costumes that would make even Erica green with envy.

But right now, Lauren had to pull the ingredients for a clown outfit out of it—or at least the basic parts. An orange leotard might be good. Didn't she have one? Or she could dye an old leotard. That would work. She wanted her clown outfit to be a clash of colors. An eye-popping explosion. Demento the Clown. That's who she'd be.

Lutz, her big gray cat, squeezed out from under his favorite spot beneath the room's one chair. He walked over and jumped up and settled himself squarely on Lauren's chest.

Automatically, Lauren began to stroke his silky fur and he began to purr. He closed his green eyes with pleasure and dug his claws into Lauren.

"Ow," Lauren said, laughing a little. "No

claws, Lutz. Put them in the closet. Get it? Claws-et."

Lutz purred harder. "Never mind the clown outfit. I should be getting all my clothes out for tomorrow," she told him. "So I don't wake Lisa and Lacey up at four-thirty. That's never a problem for you, though, is it? You're always up and dressed and waiting for me."

Opening his green eyes, Lutz regarded her. To a noncat person, his face might have looked blank. But Lauren knew he was listening to her by the slight flicking of his ears.

Lauren turned her attention back to the closet, still petting Lutz.

Then she thought of the hall closet. It was big. And all it had in it were coats and snow boots. Her gaze traveled back to the half-open closet, jammed with clothes, jumbled with shoes.

She lifted Lutz, who flattened his ears in disapproval, and set him aside.

"I am just full of brilliant ideas today, Lutz. Did you know that? This will be the third one so far: our clown act, Beck's science report, and now this."

Lutz tucked his front paws beneath his chest and looked unimpressed.

Forty-five minutes later, Lauren opened the hall closet door with a flourish. "Check it out!"

Her mother and two sisters peered inside. Lauren's clothes, unmashed and orderly, hung along one side of the big closet. "Practically all my clothes," Lauren explained. "All the ones I could hang up. And my shoes. And I figure if we got one of those shoe thingies that you hang over the door, I could organize my shoes there and stash socks in it, too. And maybe we could even fit a little tiny set of drawers in here and I could keep clothes in that, too."

"More space in our closet for my soccer gear," said Lacey instantly.

Nodding, Mrs. Wing said, "And you don't have to wake people up to get dressed in the morning. A very good idea, Lauren. Now why didn't I think of that?"

"You're not moving out?" Lisa said, anxiously.

"No." Lauren gave her sister's shoulders a reassuring squeeze. "Just my clothes. To make more room for all your dolls' clothes."

That made Lisa giggle, a gurgle of a giggle that always made Lauren want to laugh.

What would it be like to live so far away that she couldn't hear Lisa giggle every day? Or pet Lutz while he purred? Or listen to Lacey talk at warp speed about her latest soccer hero? Or even listen to Bryan make gross food jokes at dinner?

You'd have a life on ice, Lauren thought. But off the ice—it would be like life without water.

Lauren wanted to help Courtney. But how could she help someone who didn't want to be her friend?

6

"Higher. Higher!" Coach Perry commanded. "Use your toe pick to propel you."

"I am," said Lauren through clenched teeth.

But she skated away to begin again. Why was she having so much trouble with her toe loop? In theory, it was the toe jump that was the easiest.

From her left, she sensed that Courtney had stopped working on her combination spins and was watching. Lauren flashed a glance in Courtney's direction. "You've got your fists clenched you're trying so hard," Courtney observed.

Was Courtney being helpful? Lauren thought

she noticed Courtney smirking.

Lauren's fists tightened even more. She felt her nails dig into the palms of her hands. She took a deep breath. "You're right," she said to Courtney.

She unclenched her fists. She shook her hands, willing her tense arms and shoulders to relax, too.

"Good eye, Courtney," said Coach Perry.

"Yeah. Thanks," Lauren said. Maybe Courtney was being nice.

Courtney smiled at Coach Perry. But the smile slipped and was gone as she turned back to watch Lauren.

Lauren took a deep breath and tried again. She glided backward, trying to keep her glide as straight as possible. Reaching back with the toe of her left leg, she kicked it into the ice. She pushed upward with her right leg and spun counterclockwise. She drew in her arms to make her spin tight—but she didn't clench her fists. She landed neatly on her right foot.

"Much better," Coach Perry said. "Practice this correct technique, then we will work on your combination jump."

The coach turned to Courtney.

Lauren went back and did it again. And again.

And again.

From time to time, Coach Perry would call out a correction to Lauren. But whenever Lauren stopped to catch her breath, it seemed to her that Coach Perry was only heaping compliments on Courtney.

Backward, toe pick, leap, spin, land.

"Well done, Courtney. Your spins are well-centered."

Backward, toe pick, leap, spin, land.

"Courtney, good extension of the arms."

And again.

"Lauren! The arms. Bring them in to your chest. You are jumping, not flying. Your elbows are flapping."

And again.

"Perhaps, with your flexibility, we can add a little bit of the gymnast to your spin, Courtney. It would make an interesting effect in your long program."

At the end of the lesson, Lauren's thighs felt like jelly. Her ankles burned. She felt as if she could barely raise her arms and she had to wrap both hands around her water bottle to chug the last of the juice-and-water mix she always carried.

A few feet away, Courtney bent nimbly into the first of the stretches in her post-lesson routine.

"Good work. Courtney, you had a particularly nice practice," Coach Perry said.

"Yes, I did, didn't I?" Courtney said. She gave Coach Perry a saucy smile.

Lauren was shocked. Courtney sounded so cocky. So . . . like her brother Bryan at his most obnoxious and egotistical.

But Coach Perry didn't seem to mind. To Lauren's amazement, the coach returned Courtney's smile.

"Until the next lesson, then," said the coach and headed for her office.

Lauren tried to remember that Courtney was far from home and maybe feeling like a fish out of water. But today's practice and Courtney's bragging did not help.

Unable to help herself, Lauren burst out, "Wow. Are you bragging, or what?"

Courtney looked over at Lauren as if she'd just remembered Lauren was there. "Why is it bragging if it's the truth? I had a good practice. I am a good skater."

Lauren was stumped.

"To be a winner," Courtney suddenly flashed out, "you need to walk like a winner, and talk like a winner. If you're afraid to say it aloud, you're just afraid of failing."

"That's not true," said Lauren.

Courtney shrugged. "You can be a winner. Or you can be a clown. Everybody loves a winner. Everybody loves a clown. But for me, I'd rather be a winner."

Despite her soft accent, Courtney words were hard as nails, colder than the ice. There was something a little frightening about the way she spoke so calmly, matching her words to her stretches.

And why was she talking about clowns? It was spooky, almost as if she'd overheard the conversation among Lauren, Danielle, and

Annie the day before. Lauren hadn't even told Coach Perry about her plans for the clown act yet.

Lauren snapped, "I'm not a clown. I won at Regionals."

Unexpectedly, Courtney smiled. "See? That's not bragging. Is it? It's just fact."

"Yes. No. I don't know."

The smile left Courtney's face. She said, "This is a fact, too. Next time, *I'm* going to win."

Lauren watched Courtney walk away to do her stretches. Had the fish become a shark?

Annie pushed off and extended her arm in front of her. She was clutching a big, plastic flower. She leaned farther and farther forward, as if she was trying to sniff it.

Her balance became precarious. She waved her arms and her extended leg. The leg she was balanced on wobbled.

Then she fell.

Behind her, Danielle and Lauren copied all her moves and fell, too.

PLACE STAMP HERE

FLOWER POWER

Michelle Kwan won the Gold Medal at Skate America 2000 in Colorado Springs, Colorado. It was the fifth time she won the competition.

Skating Dreams #5: The Winning Edge

Skating Dreams is published by **VOLO** Hyperion.
All rights reserved.

Photo © 2001 by Dave Black

Then they spent a few seconds trying to help each other up and falling on top of one another.

After that, breathless and laughing, they skated back to the rink's edge to drink some water.

"So far so good," Annie said with satisfaction.

"So good so far," quipped Danielle. "We do make excellent clowns, I have to admit."

Lauren remembered what Courtney had said about clowns. What a nasty person she was, thought Lauren. So arrogant.

Such a good skater, too. The thought came into Lauren's mind unwelcomed.

But that didn't make Courtney a nicer person, Lauren argued with herself.

Courtney wasn't being mean when she said that about clowns and winners, Lauren continued the silent argument. *She didn't even know about your clown act. She was just being truthful, saying what she thought.*

But did she have to say it so—bluntly? And did she have to say that part about beating Lauren next time?

No. Still, didn't Lauren feel the same way? Even if she didn't say it, didn't she feel the exact same way?

"Lauren? Your turn to lead," Annie said.

"Put some good moves on us," Danielle added.

Lauren brought her attention back to the Pine Creek rink with a snap. It was no good thinking about Courtney now. Now she had a clown act to think about.

I can be a winner *and* a clown, thought Lauren.

She turned to face Annie and Danielle and began to skate backward, sticking her rear end way up in the air, with her hands on her hips.

"We have to find some music for this," she said, lifting up one foot and grabbing her toe.

"My house. Tomorrow afternoon. The land of ten thousand CDs," Danielle said. "OOOF!"

Lauren had stopped.

Annie had crashed into her.

Danielle, talking and not paying attention,

had *really* crashed into the other two. All three went down.

"Ice Crash Test Dummies," Danielle said, sitting up. "That *definitely* has to be the name of our act."

7

If you knew how to fall, it didn't hurt so much. Lauren had learned that early in her skating career. She couldn't make the ice softer, although she could make her landings lower-impact.

Sometimes.

But she'd never, even in her worst practice, deliberately fallen in so many ways and so often. Muscles ached that had never ached before. She and Annie and Danielle had practiced all that Saturday morning. Now she was going to rest—until Monday at least.

"I'm going to have to borrow Bryan's hockey pads," she muttered as she walked stiffly up to Rebecca's front door. Then she made a face. It wasn't a bad idea, not only for practice, but for the clown outfit. She wondered if some of his hockey gear would stay on without falling off. It would look pretty ridiculous.

She'd look like a total clown.

She still hadn't told Coach Perry—or Courtney—about the clown act. She'd have to, soon. She thought Coach Perry would think it was a fine idea. Coach Knudson, who taught Annie and Danielle, had thought so.

But Lauren wasn't sure she wanted to hear what Courtney had to say.

She rang the doorbell and heard the scrabbling of dog feet and excited barking. "Hey, guys," she said through the door. "It's me."

Rebecca opened the door a minute later. She was holding the dogs' two red leashes and both dachshunds were leaping around her so frantically that they were a blur.

"Okay, okay, settle down, guys," Rebecca said, handing one of the leashes to Lauren.

Lauren bent to hook the leash to Clyde's collar. She frowned. "Wow," she said. "Clyde's lost a ton of weight!"

"The no cat-food diet," Rebecca said, trying to hold Alice still long enough to snap the leash to her collar.

Running her hand down the wriggling dachshund's back, Lauren noticed how brittle his fur felt—not soft as it usually did. And she could feel his ribs.

"Uh, Beck? Don't you think it's time you took him off his diet?"

"We have. I mean, we've started giving him more food. Even a little wet food, 'cause he's been drinking so much water."

As if the word water had given Clyde an idea, he lurched forward and practically dragged Lauren out the front door and down the front steps where he immediately lifted his leg on one of the rocks lining the front walk.

He did the same thing at the end of the driveway, too, panting and pulling on his leash.

"Whoa, Clyde," Lauren said.

Rebecca and Alice raced to catch up. "We'll take them on a good long walk today. "Let's go over to the school. I brought their tennis balls and we can let them run on the fenced-in part by the track."

"Okay," Lauren agreed.

They turned in the direction of the school. After only a few hundred yards, Clyde stopped. He swung his head from side to side as if he smelled something. But his nose wasn't twitching.

"Clyde," Lauren said. "Come on, boy."

A shudder shook Clyde's body. Then his short legs folded up under him and fell over onto the sidewalk.

"Clyde?" Rebecca turned.

"Clyde. Hey, get up," Lauren said, pulling a little on the leash.

But Clyde just lay there, his eyes open and dazed looking, his ribs heaving.

"Clyde! Clyde, get up!" Rebecca shrieked. She dropped to her knees beside the fallen dog.

Clyde didn't seem to hear her.

Rebecca's face had gone pale as she stared down at her dog. Then she handed Alice's leash to Lauren. Speaking with amazing calmness she said, "Run back to the house and tell my Dad what happened. We have to go straight to the veterinarian's. Tell him it's an emergency."

Lauren stood, still shocked, Clyde's leash dangling from her nerveless fingers.

Rebecca took Clyde's leash out of Lauren's hand and let it drop. Then with amazing strength, strength Lauren never suspected in her serious, unathletic best friend, Rebecca bent, put her arms under Clyde's head and body, and stood up.

"Go!" she commanded Lauren.

This time, Lauren obeyed, running as fast as she had ever run in her life, with Alice racing alongside.

Dr. Shaw came into the waiting room. She was a tall, striking, competent-looking doctor. Lauren felt a sense of confidence just looking at Dr. Shaw.

Rebecca, Lauren, and Mr. Meyers sat in a row on the sofa at one end of the small waiting room. It had seemed like hours since they'd rushed in, with Mr. Meyers cradling Clyde in his arms. He'd called to say they were on the way, and Dr. Shaw had been waiting for them.

Lauren glanced at the clock. Not even two hours had passed since she and Rebecca and Alice and Clyde had set out on their walk to the schoolyard. But it had felt like much, much longer.

Dr. Shaw didn't bend down or try to talk baby talk to Rebecca the way some doctors might have. She sat down next to Rebecca and said, "Clyde's condition is serious. I think we've got him stabilized, but I'd like to keep him for a few days to make sure."

Rebecca blinked back tears. "Is he going to die?"

"Not if I can help it," said Dr. Shaw. "He's a young healthy dog—with just one problem."

"What is it, doctor?" Mr. Meyers leaned forward to pat Rebecca's hand.

"Diabetes. Clyde has diabetes. Have you noticed that he has seemed unusually thirsty lately?"

"Yes!" Rebecca exclaimed. "But I just thought it was because of the new dry dog food we'd bought for him. For his diet."

"Well, being overweight isn't good for any dog," said Dr. Shaw. "Clyde's weight loss is excessive, however, which is also characteristic of diabetes, as well as a stress to his system."

"I didn't know!" Rebecca almost wailed. "Oh, Clyde! It's all my fault."

"No, it's not!" her father said. "Not for a minute."

"It's nobody's fault," Dr. Shaw said. "It just happened."

Rebecca sniffled. Lauren felt helpless.

Dr. Shaw said, "Look at me, Rebecca."

Slowly Rebecca looked up.

"It's not your fault. You didn't cause Clyde to have diabetes. It just happened. Okay?"

"Really?"

"Really," said Dr. Shaw.

"Okay," said Rebecca. She straightened her shoulders. "What do we do now?"

Dr. Shaw smiled a little, and Lauren felt more hopeful. The doctor said gently, "There's nothing you can do right now except hope for the best. We're working to keep Clyde stable. After that, we'll work on figuring out the right diet and insulin dose for him. But we can talk about that later."

"In the meantime?" Mr. Meyers asked.

"In the meantime, go home and get some rest. We'll talk again tomorrow. I should know more then," said Dr. Shaw. She stood up and shook hands with all three of them.

Rebecca left the hospital reluctantly. "I hate to leave Clyde all alone," she said.

"He'll be all right," her father assured her. "I know he will. Come on. We need to let your mother know what's happening. She's still at work, and she's probably worried sick."

Rebecca nodded. But Lauren could tell that she wasn't comforted. The only thing that would comfort Rebecca would be knowing for sure, for absolute sure, that the little dog would recover.

And only time could give Rebecca that answer.

8

"Lauren?" Rebecca's voice came out the darkness. "Are you asleep?"

Curled in the trundle bed next to Rebecca's, Lauren had forced herself to lie still, so she wouldn't disturb Rebecca. She'd asked Rebecca to sleep over at her house, but Rebecca had wanted to be home in case anyone called about Clyde. So Lauren had stayed over at Rebecca's.

It had not been their usual sleepover. They'd popped popcorn, but instead of staying up late to watch videos, they'd spent the evening looking up diabetes in all the animal health books in the Meyerses' library and downloading information on the computer. Lauren's head reeled with facts, many of which she wasn't sure she understood.

But she wasn't surprised that Rebecca did. By the time Rebecca went back to Dr. Shaw's veterinary hospital to talk to her about Clyde's diabetes, Rebecca would probably know almost as much as the doctor.

"No," Lauren said. "I'm not asleep."

"Do you think Clyde's really going to be okay?" The confident Rebecca, head of her own research team of one, was gone. She sounded much younger. And frightened.

"Yes," said Lauren.

"People can die of diabetes," Rebecca said, her voice small. "The research said so."

"Not if they're taking care of themselves," Lauren said, with greater confidence than she felt. In the dark, doubts had crept back into her mind just as they must have for Rebecca. Suppose the doctor was just saying all the right things to comfort Rebecca? Suppose Clyde took a turn for the worse? Doctors weren't always right. Nobody was.

Echoing Lauren's thoughts, Rebecca said,

"What if Dr. Shaw is wrong? What if Clyde . . . what if he doesn't make it?"

"He will," said Lauren.

"You think?"

"I know," said Lauren, making herself sound fierce and sure. "I know it for a fact."

"Okay," said Rebecca.

They were silent again. After a long, long time, Lauren thought she heard sniffling from Rebecca's bed.

Lauren sat up. "Hot chocolate," she said into the darkness. "Why don't we make some?" She reached out and switched on the bedside lamp.

Rebecca sat up too. Sheepishly, she wiped tears from her cheeks. "Okay," she said. "Only, can I have mint tea with honey?"

"Sure. Come on," Lauren commanded. She pretended she didn't notice the tears. If Rebecca needed to cry on Lauren's shoulder, she would. Right now, she just wanted to be brave, and logical, and sure that Clyde would be fine.

Lauren made Rebecca sit down at the kitchen table while she boiled water for tea. As Lauren poured out the tea and set out the honey and spoons, she kept up a flow of talk. "You know what, you still have to keep Alice on her diet. And you should probably make a list of questions for Dr. Shaw. That way, she won't waste time telling you stuff you already know."

"A list," said Rebecca. "That's a good idea." Her voice took on a little more animation.

"Why don't you start it now?" Lauren grabbed the phone notebook on the counter and shoved it and a pen across the table to Rebecca.

"Okay," said Rebecca. The scientist in her took over. She picked up the pen and, reading aloud as she wrote, printed "#1" at the top of the page.

"Is it possible to control diabetes by diet alone?"

"Good question," said Lauren.

Rebecca looked up. She smiled a shadow smile. "Thanks, Lauren," she said.

Lauren smiled back. "Hey," she said. "What are best friends since first grade for? Now, I have a question. Why does having diabetes make a dog so thirsty?"

"Good question," Rebecca said back, and began to write.

"A clown act?" Coach Perry smiled. "Coach Knudson *did* mention something about that to me."

"I thought she might have," Lauren said. She yawned hugely. After staying awake most of Saturday night with Rebecca, she'd slept like a rock the Sunday night. That morning, the sound of the alarm in the predawn darkness had come much too soon.

Lauren had stopped her warm-up loops a loop early to talk to Coach Perry. Across the rink, Courtney glided along with seeming effortlessness. Lauren never felt like that when she was warming up. Maybe, she thought, Courtney warmed up before she even got to the rink.

Hmmm.

"It's a clever idea," the coach said. "I'll be interested to see your performance. But I think you should also do a short, serious piece."

"Like my short program?" Lauren asked.

"Or a segment of the long program. Not too

much. Just to give the audience an idea of what figure skaters do that hockey players do not." Coach Perry smiled.

"I can do that," Lauren agreed. "I could do my long program up to the double-double, and end with a Hamill camel."

The coach nodded. "I like it."

Courtney swooshed by, giving them a brief, sideways glance.

Lauren knew without asking that Courtney was doing a short, *serious* performance at the celebration. She said, "We're going to do a run-through of the Ice Crash Test Dummies—that's the name of our clown act—for Coach Knudson next Saturday morning early at the Pine Creek rink. When the rink just opens and there aren't lots of people on the ice. I mean, if you'd like to see it."

"I'll be there," said Coach Perry.

"Great," said Lauren. "We'll appreciate any help we can get."

Courtney skated back to them and stopped. She looked from Coach Perry to Lauren. "Is this a secret meeting?" she asked.

The coach's eyebrows went up. "No secrets," she said. "We're making plans for the Arena opening celebration."

Courtney raised her own eyebrows in unconscious imitation of Coach Perry. "What do you have planned, Lauren?"

"Oh, I've got a plan," Lauren said. She smiled back, thinking of the clown suit she was making, piece by piece, from all the odds and ends of clothes and equipment in her family's house. "And it's a winner."

Lauren paused. "Just like your program," she said. "Well, our program isn't exactly like yours. Not the one Annie, Danielle, and I are doing. But I'm sure yours is a winner, too."

Courtney looked confused, then suspicious. "Are you making fun of me?" she demanded.

"No," said Lauren. "I was paying you a compliment, actually."

"Oh," said Courtney. She frowned. Then she said, reluctantly, "Thanks. I think."

"You're welcome," Lauren said cheerfully. Then she pushed off to finish her warm-up loops.

* * *

Rebecca was waiting for Lauren at her locker when she arrived after first period. "Clyde?" Lauren asked, breathlessly.

"The same," Rebecca said. "Stable. Well, maybe a little better. Dr. Shaw is a very cautious person, you know."

"Which means until Clyde is *way* better, she won't say anything, right?" Lauren stuffed books in her locker, shifted notebooks.

"Right," said Rebecca. "But I'm not as worried. See, if he'd been going to, you know, die, or anything, he'd have done already, don't you think?"

"I think," agreed Lauren. "You know what, Rebecca? You'd make a good veterinarian. Or doctor. You were so calm on Saturday when Clyde got sick."

Rebecca nodded matter-of-factly. "It's on my list of possible careers," she said.

For a moment, Rebecca reminded Lauren strongly of—who?

Courtney. Courtney the confident. Or Courtney the cocky.

Lauren had to smile. Never in a thousand

years, no matter what Rebecca said, would Lauren think of her as cocky or arrogant.

Just, *right*. Rebecca the right.

And what was wrong with that?

"What? Why are you smiling like that?" Rebecca asked.

Slamming her locker, Lauren hoisted her pack and pretended to stagger. The clown act was beginning to take over her into her everyday life.

"I'm counting what you said as good news," Lauren told Rebecca. "That's why I'm smiling. Listen, we're having a dress rehearsal of our clown act next Saturday morning. Eight-thirty, when the Pine Creek rink opens. You should be there."

"Okay," said Rebecca. "Okay, I will."

Lauren stared at herself in the mirror. She wrinkled her nose. "These shoulder pads stink!"

"No, they don't," Bryan said. He was leaning against the doorjamb, watching the clown costume session. "They were washed years ago. Before they got put away. Right, Mom?"

"We'll wash them again," Mrs. Wing promised. "Stand *still*, Lauren."

The command was a familiar one, the cry of every costume fitting which Lauren had ever endured. This fitting, however, was not in any other way like any other costume fitting Lauren had ever had. No gauze, no lace, no silky material to shift and pin and hold up to the light. When she looked in the mirror, she didn't see a fairy princess, an ice queen, a figure skating goddess-to-be.

No. She saw a scarecrow of a hockey player.

For her clown act, Lauren had chosen to be Demento the Hockey Player. She was wearing as many pieces of one of Bryan's old hockey uniforms as she could get to stay on. Huge shoulder pads sprouted like wings from her shoulders. Her thighs looked like big pillows. To one side of the mirror on the floor was an old helmet to which Lauren had glued an assortment of flowers, fake papier-mâché birds and butterflies.

Bryan glanced at the helmet from time to time with an expression of disgust on his face.

But he didn't comment.

Mrs. Wing was pinning up the pants so she could hem them. She was also going to sew flower and butterfly appliqués on the pants and the shirt.

Lauren hadn't told Bryan that part, yet.

"What about Annie and Danielle?" Bryan asked. "Are they gonna look this goofy?"

"I hope so. We're a clown act," Lauren said.

"You can say that again." Bryan snorted.

Lauren smiled.

The clown in the mirror smiled back.

But the clown act was just that, Lauren told herself. An act.

It didn't prove that she wasn't serious, that she didn't have what it took to take that win at Regionals and go all the way to the top.

Only someone who is really good can do a clown act, she told herself.

Only the best.

And I'm the best, she told herself. The best clown.

The best skater.

No matter what Courtney or anyone says.

9

The phone rang as Lauren was decorating Bryan's old hockey stick. She was using glitter nail polish to give added sparkle to the butterfly decals.

"Lauren! For you!" Lauren's mother came to the door of the family room holding the phone.

Lauren laid the hockey stick carefully on a high shelf of the family room bookcase, where neither Lisa nor, she hoped, Lutz, could get to it. Then she took the phone.

"He's okay!" Rebecca said. "He's coming home tomorrow. We're going to get him tomorrow. At lunch. Mom's getting me out of school to do it."

"Clyde's okay? Oh, Beck, that's the best news ever!"

"I'm typing out all the questions I have about diabetes. I'm going to start a computer database for Clyde's diabetes. You know, this could . . ."

"Make an interesting science project," Lauren finished for Rebecca. She laughed.

Rebecca laughed, too. "I bet Clyde never thought he was a scientific dog."

"A scientific dachshund," Lauren corrected.

They talked for a few minutes longer. Lauren clicked the phone off with a huge smile on her face. "Good for you, Clyde," she said aloud. "Good boy."

Then she flipped through her book of stickers. There it was. A dachshund sticker on a page of dog stickers. Lauren peeled it off and stuck to the top of the hockey stick in honor of Clyde.

"Music," commanded Annie grandly.

Her older sister Moira pressed the play button on the tape player. The arena had a sound system, but it was closed at the moment, and they were making do with the old boom box.

Annie sprinted out onto the ice, pretended to trip, and slid across on her belly. She was dressed in layers and layers of clothes. When she fell, a quick, hidden twitch of her hand made one leg of the top pair of pants pull free.

Annie was wearing tie-dyed red boxer shorts over her acid-pink leotard and yellow-and-blue-striped tights. At the end of the program, the rest of her clothes would be scattered from one end of the rink to the other. She was the Fashion Victim clown.

Danielle had chosen the Goofy Princess look: a tiara tipped precariously off long fake black hair. Enormous eyelashes and sequined eyebrows framed her eyes. She was wearing a pink tutu: stiff layers of net sticking out around her. She was also wearing what looked like the entire collection of costume jewelry from a department store. As a final touch, Danielle had blacked out her two front teeth.

As Lauren—Demento the Hockey Player—waited for her music cue, she laughed at her two friends. When she stepped onto the ice to join them, she pretended to trip over her hockey stick and did a near face plant on the ice.

The routine looked wild and crazy, Lauren knew. But the three of them had been rehearsing it down to the last leap and tumble. They raced around the ice, scrambling, falling, crashing, pointing at one another in exaggerated outrage and blame. They played snap-the-whip and sent Danielle spinning off until it seemed as if she was about to go flying into the stands.

As the music reached the end, the Ice Crash Test Dummies began to take frantic, dramatic bows at center ice, only to knock each other down one final time.

The music they'd chosen was "Bolero"—the same piece that the famous ice dancers Torvill and Dean had used to skate to gold and push pairs performance boundaries at the 1984 Winter Olympics. As Torvill and Dean had done, Lauren, Danielle, and Annie ended stretched out dramatically on the ice.

Lauren had thought she'd feel foolish.

But the laughter and applause as the tape ended was music to her ears.

Coach Knudson was applauding and shaking her head as they got up. Coach Perry, who was sitting next to her, was also applauding. "That was wonderful!" Coach Knudson exclaimed. "Who's idea was it to use 'Bolero'?"

"Mine," said Danielle.

"Bravo," said Coach Perry, nodding approvingly.

"You guys were amazing," said Rebecca. "I knew you could skate, but I never knew you could skate that bad. Or do I mean good?"

"It's harder than you'd think, trying to do things together," Annie said. She shook her head. "I don't see how the pairs skaters do it."

"I didn't think it was so hard," protested Danielle.

Lauren pretended to swipe at Danielle with her stick. Danielle, never one to pass up a dramatic moment, promptly fell back on the ice and stuck her skates in the air.

"Well, Coach Perry, Coach Knudson?" Lauren said. "Any suggestions, tips . . ."

Her voice trailed off. Sitting higher up in the stands was Courtney and a compact woman with red-brown hair and straight eyebrows that were almost exactly like Courtney's.

As Lauren stared in dismay, Courtney and the woman stood up and walked down the steps to join everyone else.

Coach Perry looked from Lauren to Courtney and back as Courtney stopped in front of Lauren.

"Oh!" said Lauren, remembering her manners. "Uh, Courtney. Courtney Reeves, these are my best skating buddies, Danielle and Annie. And this is Coach Knudson, who coached me and still coaches Danielle and Annie. And this is my best friend since first grade, Rebecca, who is *not* a figure skater." She stopped.

"Don't worry," Rebecca said. "We won't give you a test on remembering our names. It's nice to meet you. Lauren says you're a great skater."

Lauren blinked. Had she said that?

Annie was nodding and smiling, too.

"My aunt." Courtney spoke at last. "Caroline Bingham."

"Ms. Bingham." Coach Knudson was holding out her hand.

"So you're staying with your aunt," said Annie. "How do you like it?"

The familiar guarded look flashed into Courtney's eyes. "It's okay," she said. She shrugged. Today, in jeans and a rugby shirt, she still looked very fashionable.

"You've got a dog?" Danielle asked.

"Yeah . . . I guess Lauren told you," Courtney said.

"Well, Rebecca's a real dog fanatic. Dogs come up a lot in Lauren's conversations, too, in case you haven't noticed," Danielle said.

"Uh, no. I hadn't noticed." Courtney's head was moving back and forth, as if she was watching a tennis match.

"Are you, like, camped on e-mail to all your friends back home?" Annie inquired.

Courtney shrugged. "Some," she said. "I didn't have that many friends. I concentrated on my skating."

That stopped the conversation.

"I'm glad you could make it, Courtney, and meet everyone," Coach Perry said.

"We're glad, too," Ms. Bingham said. "Since

my promotion, I've worked so much that I feel like Courtney spends all her time alone or with the baby-sitter. I'm glad she has you as a friend, Lauren."

"Aunt Carol," Courtney said, trying to head her aunt off.

Friend? Me? Lauren almost blurted the words out.

"Courtney's talked so much about you. I know how you inspire her to work her hardest," Courtney's aunt went on.

"She inspires me, too," Lauren said, since Ms. Bingham clearly expected her to say something.

Ms. Bingham beamed. "Well, we'd better be going. I've got Saturday chores to do. Unless you want to stay here with your friends, Courtney? I could pick you up after I . . ."

"I'll go with you," Courtney interrupted. "They have to practice."

Danielle frowned. The way Courtney had said it, it had sounded as if the clown act needed work.

Had she meant it that way?

Lauren knew what Danielle was thinking. She'd thought the same thing herself. But she was more used to Courtney's way of speaking now. It didn't sound as harsh to Lauren.

And even if she had meant to take a shot, what difference did it make?

Still, she couldn't resist needling Courtney, just a little. "You could practice, too, Courtney," Lauren said. She hadn't said that Courtney needed practice, either. But some *might* interpret it that way.

Courtney met Lauren's eyes. She half-smiled. "Thanks," she said. "But no thanks."

"See you Monday, then," Lauren said. She watched as Courtney and her aunt left. Her aunt gestured and talked as they walked away. Courtney nodded, appearing to say very little.

So maybe Courtney was blunt and short-spoken with everyone, not just Lauren.

"I'm going to go hang out with Alice and Clyde," Rebecca said.

"I'll come by later," Lauren promised.

"Later," agreed Rebecca. "Don't practice too

much. I don't think I can laugh any harder than I already did."

Danielle promptly took a bow—and fell forward in a heap.

10

The day before the big skating event, Lauren was having a bad day.

She kept stepping out of jumps. One arm and then the other would seem to develop a mind of its own, and go flying out when she did a spin.

She fell. Repeatedly.

Scrambling up from the ice, Lauren tried to get back up, quickly, and begin again.

"Concentrate," Coach Perry intoned.

"I *am* concentrating," Lauren said. She sounded frustrated.

Then, as Lauren fell out of a toe loop, Coach Perry said, "Stop."

Both Lauren and Courtney looked at the coach in surprise.

"Stop?" said Lauren, as if Coach Perry had spoken in another language.

"Yes. You are practicing your mistakes. What good is that?" Coach Perry asked.

Lauren felt her face turn bright red. She couldn't look at Courtney. She was probably smiling a smug grin. Lauren knew that she could do her short, short piece flawlessly.

"I can do this," Lauren said.

"No. Single-single combination," Coach Perry commanded.

"What?" Again, Lauren looked as if she couldn't quite believe her ears.

"Basic. Basics are what you build on," Coach Perry said.

Lauren extended her arm and her leg, leaned forward, and carved a perfect figure on the ice.

"Bad practice, good show," Courtney said, after practice.

"That's what my old coach used to say," she went on as Lauren bent into her post-practice stretches. "She always says when a dress rehearsal goes all wrong, right before opening night, it means the skate will go perfectly."

"Mmm," Lauren said. She straightened up. "Well, that means I'm going to have a great performance at the opening, then."

"Well, you are the champion," Courtney said and then turned around to do her own stretching.

"Right," Lauren said. But she sure didn't feel like a winning champion.

Ears flying, Clyde and Alice both raced toward Lauren. Clyde beat Alice by a tongue and began giving Lauren's ear a vigorous washing.

"Good boy," Lauren crooned. "Good boy, Clyde." She grabbed Clyde and held him at arm's length. "He really does look great, Beck."

"He's himself again," Rebecca said. "I don't think he even remembers getting sick."

"I'll never forget it," Lauren said.

Rebecca picked up the tennis ball and threw it. The dogs raced away.

"What's the plan? What do you have to do for Clyde now?" Lauren asked.

"He has a special diet, which means that Alice is pretty much on the same diet." Rebecca shrugged. "It's basically just a healthy one, no fruit treats, things like that. His meals are divided up into two a day, to help keep his blood sugar level. No sweets."

"You never gave the dogs sweets, anyway," Lauren said.

"No. But that's just what Dr. Shaw said. And Clyde gets an insulin shot every morning after breakfast. And for a while, we have to take him in and get his blood checked to make sure that the insulin is the right dose. That's something we'll always have to watch."

"It doesn't sound so bad," Lauren said.

"It's not. Clyde doesn't even know. I gave him his insulin shot this morning and he just looked around like, what's that?"

"You gave Clyde his shot? You are so brave, Beck. I could never do that in a million years."

Rebecca said, "Sure you could. If Lutz needed it, you'd do it."

"I don't know. Maybe."

They sat in comfortable silence for a while,

watching the dogs play. Lauren told Rebecca about her morning practice with Courtney.

"I can't believe she said that to me," Lauren said.

"She's pretty prickly," Rebecca said. "But you have to admit, it was a logical thing to say."

"I admit it. But I don't like it." Lauren sighed. "If she doesn't watch it, I'm going to stop being nice."

"No you won't," said Rebecca. "Just like you're not going to stop being the best skater. No matter what anyone says."

"Yeah. Okay," Lauren said.

"I wonder why she does that?" Rebecca said. "I mean, it's not even a contest or anything. You're just skating for fun tomorrow."

"Maybe I am. But I don't think Courtney is. You know, for her, everything is a contest, I think. Every practice. Every lesson."

"Yuck," said Rebecca. Her eyes followed Clyde and Alice as they began to dig at a clump of clover.

"She's so competitive," agreed Lauren. She didn't say "Poor Courtney." She didn't feel sorry for Courtney anymore. Courtney was tough and talented.

Courtney was a winner. She loved to skate and to compete.

Just like me, Lauren thought. She sighed again. This time it was a sigh of contentment.

How quickly things had changed, how easily she had allowed her belief in herself and her dreams to be shaken, Lauren thought. She'd won at Regionals, had been set to go to Sectionals brimming with confidence. She was becoming the figure skater she knew she could be.

And then Courtney had come along and undermined Lauren's confidence just like that. Almost—but not quite—Courtney had ruined the winning edge that Lauren had been skating on.

Only it wasn't Courtney who had done it, Lauren realized now. She had let it happen. She had done it to herself.

Out of the turmoil of the past few weeks, Lauren had learned that being a winner didn't mean just coming in first place. It meant being there for her friends. It meant believing in herself.

"What are you thinking about?" Rebecca asked.

"That I feel pretty." Lauren paused. "Pretty good."

"Go, gogogogogo!" Annie was practically jumping out of the bleachers with excitement.

Below, Bryan Wing, hockey king, was skimming the puck left and right across the ice with seemingly casual flicks of his stick.

He faked. Then he flipped a pass to his wing.

The goalie never had a chance.

"Hooray!" Shrieking, Annie leaped to her feet, along with the rest of the spectators crowding into the Silver Springs Arena.

A few minutes later, the Otters won their game.

Annie put two fingers in her mouth and let

out a piercing whistle. Lacey joined in and the two were off on a chorus of teakettle notes that made Lisa clap her hands over her ears.

Mr. and Mrs. Wing and Lauren, Rebecca, and Danielle settled for applauding.

Lauren had skated in an event at the arena before, but she'd never seen it so dressed up. Flags hung from the rafters. Bunting was draped across every entrance. And what seemed like more and more people kept coming and going.

The announcer called a lunch break and promised "some great figure skating performances when you get back."

Danielle nudged Annie. "That's us," she said.

"We're only one of the acts," Lauren reminded her.

"Actually, four of the acts," Danielle said. "If you count the shorts medley. We're each doing a short piece in that, and then the clown act. That makes four acts."

Lauren felt a twist of nervousness inside. Danielle, who seemed to have been born to be the center of attention, appeared perfectly cool and calm. She chatted on, teasing Lisa and Lacey, making sly references to Bryan that brought a rush of color to Annie's cheeks.

Mrs. Wing unpacked the picnic basket that Mr. Wing had put together and passed around sandwiches and fruit. The McGraths arrived to join them, followed by Danielle's parents.

Bryan was the last to arrive. His hair was wet from the shower and he had a butterfly Band-Aid on his chin.

Annie said, "Oh! Does it hurt?"

"What?" said Bryan, looking pleased with himself.

"Your chin," Annie said.

"It's broken!" said Lisa.

"Not broken, Lisa," Rebecca reassured her. "Just cut."

"No worries, Lisa. It's nothing," Bryan said. "All in a day's work. You figure skaters don't know how easy you have it."

"Have a sandwich," Mrs. Wing said.

"Yeah. That way, your mouth can keep moving, but you won't be saying dumb, totally untrue things," Lauren added.

Bryan grinned. "Okay, okay."

Suddenly Danielle giggled.

"What?" asked Lacey. "What's so funny?"

"Can you imagine figure skaters armed with hockey sticks? Giving each other full body checks?"

"It would change the judging. Definitely," Annie said, her own face breaking into a grin.

"Or if Erica came around. Boom. One good block onto the boards and she'd be *history*," Annie said.

"Not Erica. She'd come out mad and ready for revenge," Danielle said.

"Now that would be something to see," Bryan put in between enormous bites of his second sandwich. "A bench-clearing figure skaters fight. Hey! You guys are all skating together today, right? It could happen!"

Lauren looked around the hallway just outside the entrance to the ice at the far end of the rink. Out in the arena, the lights dimmed. A tall, skinny man with a clipboard and shirt that said OFFICIAL spoke urgently into his phone, clipped to his belt, and then shouted, "OKAY, PEOPLE. LISTEN UP."

The noise level dropped.

"One more time. Each skater goes out as his or her name is called. You know the order. If you can't remember, the list is posted over there on the wall." He pointed. Heads turned.

"On the ice, skate as if you were warming up for an event. It will be crowded. Don't crash into each other. And make it look good. After approximately one minute, we will retreat from the ice in the same order we entered it. Then the lights will go down and each skater will enter the rink for his or her short skate as the name is called. You will be spotlighted to center rink. Then the lights will go up again. Got it?"

Murmurs broke out. But not questions. Lauren was surrounded by skaters who knew their jobs on the ice.

The music blared, then went silent. The crowd noise went from loud cacaphony to expectant hum.

"Okay," said the official. "One, two, three . . ."

* * *

Lauren gulped down water. The opening had gone well. No skater crashes or even near misses—and lots and lots of applause from the crowd.

Now they would skate in order, each skater performing a short, short piece. Lauren would be the third skater on, followed by Danielle and Annie. That was to give them time to get into their clown costumes.

Then they would head back out onto the ice to provide some comic relief.

After that would come more skaters, including Courtney. Then back out on to the ice as a group, lined up this time holding on to one another. As names were called, each skater would slip out of the line, do a spin or leap or other trick, and then line up at center ice.

All in a line at the end, they'd take their bows.

"I think they like us," Danielle said.

Courtney's dark red hair bobbed into view, then disappeared. She was in the corner, and Lauren knew instantly that Courtney was stretching.

She'd barely had time to do more than nod at Courtney. The girl's face had been pale and tight, making the bright makeup that looked so good on the ice and so extreme and clownlike off it seem even more overdone: red spots of color on her cheekbones, slashes of emerald eye shadow that matched her outfit, a sprinkling of glitter in her shining hair.

Lauren clumped over. "Looking good," she said.

Courtney bobbed up, then down, reaching for her ankle propped on the railing.

"I guess," she muttered.

Raising her eyebrows in surprise, Lauren said, "You guess?"

Still stretching, Courtney managed to shrug. "It's not like it's a real competition," she said. It was as if she was trying to reassure herself.

"True. So have fun," Lauren said.

"Fun," said Courtney. It was that "what is that, another language?" tone of voice.

"Fun," repeated Lauren firmly. She gave Courtney her "Give me a six, judge" center-ice special smile and went back to join her friends.

Then the announcer was calling her name.

Lauren flew out onto the ice. Her grin broadened as she heard the piercing whistle from the stands where her family sat. Lacey and Bryan, she guessed, giving her a whistle concert.

She danced across the blue-white surface. Her outfit was an old one, a solid black dress.

Her program was perfect. Courtney was right about bad rehearsals and perfect shows. With each move, Lauren felt more comfortable. She was having fun. She did have a winning edge. After all . . . it was her love of skating.

Her program ended with more piercing whistles and a satisfying roar of applause—and an inward sigh of relief.

Annie burst past Lauren as she stepped out of the rink. Dressed in bright red, she seemed to blaze across the ice.

Danielle moaned, "I *have* to go to the bathroom."

"No, you don't," Lauren said. "You just think you do. You always think you do right before you go on."

"I do. I do," Danielle insisted. But she stayed

where she was.

Danielle was as elegant as ever. Lauren could tell the audience was impressed. On the ice, Danielle had the poise and grace of a much older skater.

But her first words off the ice were far from poised. "Bathroom!" she gasped.

"And clown outfits," agreed Annie. "Let's go!"

12

The hockey pads burst out of Lauren's locker as if they were doing their own clown act.

"Ahhh!" exclaimed Lauren. She scooped them up and began her transformation into Demento the Hockey Player.

It seemed to take forever. Lauren strained to hear the announcer's voice as she wrestled with the thigh pads and tight pants that held them in place.

"Three minutes," Annie announced, looking at the travel alarm clock she'd tucked onto the top shelf of her locker.

"Lipstick! My lipstick!" Danielle made a dive as it rolled away under a bench.

Finally, they were clopping back down the hall in their skate guards at top speed. Laughter followed them as they reached the skaters waiting near the entrance.

They would go on as soon as the skater on the ice now finished.

Lauren took a deep breath.

Danielle said, "I look *terrible*."

"Funny," corrected Annie. "And that's the point."

Lauren glanced around at the other skaters in their shimmering, glittering, floating costumes. The Ice Crash Test Dummies definitely stood out.

Her eyes met one skater's. Courtney.

Lauren smiled.

Courtney kept staring, as if she couldn't quite believe her eyes.

Suddenly, Courtney grinned.

It was so unexpected that Lauren almost did fall right there at rinkside.

Courtney never just smiled like that.

Immediately Lauren wondered if Courtney was laughing at her.

So what if she is, Lauren told herself. That's what she's supposed to do.

She gave Courtney a grin back, and big, goofy wink.

Then it was time for the Ice Crash Test Dummies to go on.

They tumbled out onto the ice to applause. The applause quickly turned into laughter.

Lauren had never had anyone laugh at her before like that—not when she was skating. For a moment, it unnerved her.

She flailed her arms and her hockey stick, spinning as if she was out of control. Danielle ducked. The hockey stick caught Annie right on her behind, sending her flying. Annie scrambled to her feet, a picture of righteous indignation.

She left behind one of her shirt sleeves. Now one arm was covered in a striped long-under-shirt sleeve.

Laughter swelled. And the sound of it was sweet.

Lauren, Annie, and Danielle ducked and wove and fell up and down the ice. When they finished, stretched out in a line just like Torvill and Dean in their "Bolero" piece, an enormous roar seemed to raise the roof.

They'd gotten a standing ovation!

Holding hands, they got to their feet and bowed. Then they swooped around the ice, gathering Annie's clothing and piling it into her arms. As they left, still staggering and weaving and pretending to almost fall, laughter followed them.

The skaters backstage were applauding, too. The pairs skaters, Yanna and Nat, were laughing and nodding.

"Tough act to follow," said Yanna.

"You were excellent," agreed Nat.

"Bravo," called another older skater.

A warm glow filled Lauren. It was true. Everybody loved a clown.

Except maybe, Courtney.

She passed without acknowledging them. Had she even seen their act?

Nevertheless, Lauren found herself holding her breath as Courtney skated. She knew how good Courtney was in lessons. But how good was she at center ice?

The answer was: good.

Very, very good.

Lauren watched her rival, her skating lesson partner, and admired the precision, the timing, the controlled recklessness of her tricks.

And yet. And yet . . .

I'm as good as Courtney is, Lauren thought. And I can be better.

She knew it deep inside. And unlike Courtney, she didn't have to say it aloud. Lauren could keep her winning edge sharp without having to talk about it to anyone else.

And then, much too quickly, it was time for the final group skate.

The Ice Crash Test Dummies had kept on their outfits. They went out together to a roar of approval. And they stayed in character to the end.

Waves of applause and showers of flowers—just like at a competition, Lauren noted with surprise—poured down on the skaters as they took their final bows.

"This," said Danielle out of the side of her incredibly bright red-lipsticked mouth, "was great. Great!"

They skated off the ice. Now the arena was no longer new, Lauren thought. Now it really did feel like home.

"Don't move," a familiar voice commanded.

The Ice Crash Test Dummies turned, and flashbulbs blinded them. Their families were leaning over the railing to preserve the moment forever. Mr. Kurowicki, as usual, had his video camera rolling.

After the skate, the locker room was filled with a jumble of noisy, cheerful skaters.

Lauren was almost sorry to take off her Demento duds. It had been so much fun.

"Hey."

Lauren looked up. It was Courtney.

"Y'all looked good," she said. She hesitated. "Really good.

"Even for clowns?" Lauren couldn't resist asking.

Courtney smiled. "Even for clowns," she said. Her eyes went from Danielle, who was scrubbing at her makeup as she peered in a mirror Annie was holding, to Annie, and back to Lauren.

She looked, Lauren thought, a little wistful.

Impulsively she said, "We'll probably go get pizza or ice cream or something. You want to come?"

Danielle and Annie had noticed Courtney now. Danielle said, "Yeah. We promise to be dressed normally by then."

Courtney hesitated. For a moment, Lauren thought she would nod, say yes.

But she didn't.

Courtney shook her head. "No thanks," she said, in her old, abrupt, almost-rude Courtney way. Then she turned and walked down the row of lockers and out of sight.

"Huh," said Annie.

"I don't get her," Danielle said. "What does she think you're going to do? What does she think will happen to her if she's a little friendly?"

"She loses her edge," Lauren said. "Maybe she can't be friends with the people she skates against. Or at least, she thinks she can't."

"Hmm," said Annie. "Uh. Ow!"

She hopped around on one foot. "I stepped on a pin or something," she said. She lost her balance, staggered, and crashed against a locker.

Both Danielle and Lauren grabbed for her.

Their heads cracked together. They reeled back as Annie toppled forward.

Lauren stood up. She put out her hand, palm up. Danielle and Annie slapped palms with her.

"Ice Crash Test Dummies rule!" said Lauren Demento Wing.

The three friends laughed. And Lauren realized that she was the luckiest skater. She had championship friends on and off the ice.

Ask Michelle!

If you have a question that you would like to ask Michelle, visit http://www.skatingdreams.com

Do you miss your family when you're away on tours and competitions?

I miss my family and friends a lot when I'm on the road. Especially on tour because I'm gone for so long. I always bring photos of everybody when I'm on tour. I am definitely a homebody, so I try to be at home as much as I can. Thank goodness for the cell phone. I can make phone calls when I'm on the bus or at the arena.

Is it harder to skate first or last in a competition?

Actually, both are difficult. It is tough skating first in a competition because you don't have much time to catch your breath after the six-minute warm-up. It's also hard skating last because you have about a forty-five-minute wait after the warm-up. You have to stay in motion and in focus.

Where do you keep your Olympic medal?

I keep my Olympic medal in a safe deposit box. I don't want to lose it because it can't be replaced.

How do you handle nervousness at a competition?

I believe the most difficult thing about competition is controlling your nerves. It's a matter of being confident when you are performing. You definitely do not want to have any doubt in your head. Practice is a place where you try and work out the kinks. Hopefully, when you are at a competition you are prepared and confident.

MICHELLE KWAN PRESENTS

Skating Dreams

Catch up on the thrills and heartbreaks of Lauren Wing with these books:

The exciting new series for the young ice-skating fan!

Collectible postcard of Michelle Kwan in each book!

SKATING DREAMS #1: *The Turning Point*

SKATING DREAMS #2: *Staying Balanced*

SKATING DREAMS #3: *Skating Backward*

SKATING DREAMS #4: *Champion's Luck*

HYPERION BOOKS FOR CHILDREN

© Disney